Bad "Bad" Hygiene

by Sonya J. Bowser
Penciled by Shiela Alejandro
Colorist: Nicholas Lonprez
Cover design by Sonya J. Bowser
Book layout & Design by Clark Kenyon

Text copyright © 2016 by Sonya J. Bowser

Illustrations copyright © by Sonya J. Bowser

www.zoliezi.com

Summary: Zolie Zi takes pride in her hygiene and is always sure to check off her daily hygiene "to do's" until she is faced with a new type of Hygiene that is not on the list. Zolie has to find out through her family and friends that something is wrong with her nose because she can't seem to smell the new smell coming from her body. Will Zolie ever smell the new smell coming from her body and add it to the Hygiene list? Or will her family and friends have to keep telling her that something is wrong with her nose?

ISBN: 978-1-5323-2180-1

[1. Schools-Fiction. 2. Friendship-Fiction]
Printed in the United States of America

First paperback edition 10 9 8 7 6 5 4 3 2 1

Acknowledgements

I would like to thank the special people who continue to love on Zolie Zi and support her books. Lillian (Mom), Benny (Dad), Patricia Broadbent (GodMother), Mecca, Shareefah, Wakeelah, Cavon, Chanel, Nikki Morgan, Towana Taylor-Jackson, L'Shonny Debousse-Young, Asia Lynn/Robert Martin and a host of family, friends and supporters. Words are not enough to express my love and thanks for all of you.

To my Z-Girl/Z-Boy Ambassadors, who mean the world to me. All of you have survived bullying or understand what to do if you are faced with bullying. Sariah Martin, Robert Martin, Amari Martin, Na'Ilah Muhammad, Maylah Chanel, Leeah D. Jackson, Jai Lee, Alani Simone, Syndey K. Green, Kennedy Hall, Drew Wiggins, Tylon Larry, Yoshi Wiggins, Caden Michael Young, Milani Trichelle, Iyana and Keyana Miller, J'Sunn Dior, Tasia Fortune, C.J. Adderly, Jada Adderly, Mariah Lambert, Alayna and last but not least, my very 1st Z-Girl, Yakini Perez!! Your support means the world to me. Love you all so much!!

I want to give a special thank you to Zoe Powell, Senior Education Officer for Guidance Counselors in the Bahamas. Thank you for welcoming Zolie Zi into the Bahamas School District and for taking the time to make sure that the students in Nassau and surrounding Islands get the chance to be inspired and empowered by the message(s) in Zolie Zi's books and curriculum. I appreciate you more than you know. Much love and respect.

A special thank you to Shazanna Muhammad, Alani Simone and Na'Ilah Muhammad for taking the time to read my second book and give me your honest feedback. You girls are the best!!

Honorable mention to all of the Z-Moms, thank you for sharing your girls with Team Zolie Zi. Thank you all and love you all!!

Last, but not least, to the Creator who gave me the vision, words, inspiration and motivation to keep doing what I love. I could never re-pay you.

Thank you!

 # Contents 

Chapter One

Good Hi-Jean (hygiene)

Hi, my name is Zolie pronounced Zo-Lee and my last name is Zi pronounced Z.

My friends call me "Ms. Chit Chat." They call me that because they say that I talk a lot. I don't think that I talk any more than they do. But, everyone has an opinion and there is nothing that I can do about that.

Oh, back to my name, I prefer that you just call me Zolie.

I go to "Helping Hands Academy for the Gifted and Talented children." Yup, that's me, gifted and talented. My teacher's name is Mrs. Mahogany and my favorite subject is Science.

Every morning when I wake up, I always jump out of bed and run to the bathroom to brush my teeth because my mom won't talk to me if my breath stinks.

She always says, "Zolie, it is rude to talk to someone with stinky breath from a tongue that has not been brushed and from teeth that have not been brushed."

And then my dad always says, "Zolie, only brush the teeth that you want to keep!!"

Then I say, "Dad, I would like to keep all of my teeth," and then he says, "Well, you better get to brushing them before you lose them all!"

So, I always remember to brush all of my teeth every day and my tongue too.

After I brush my teeth, I wash my face because my mom always says that if you brush your teeth after you wash your face, you will have a toothpaste ring all around your mouth.

One day I decided to ask her, "Mommy, what is that? What is that toothpaste ring thing??" She replied, "Zolie, it is a white ring that looks like a milk mustache, but it makes a circle around your whole mouth. It happens because the water dries around the mouth after brushing your teeth."

Then I said, "Oh, ok."

You know what? One day I decided not to wash my face after I brushed my teeth just to see what this toothpaste ring thing was that my mom was talking about and guess what? It did look just like a white milk stain around my mouth! When I looked at myself in the mirror I just laughed out loud because I looked so funny with the toothpaste ring around my mouth and I understood why my mom tells us to wash our face after brushing our teeth.

After washing my face I have to put chapstick on my lips so that they won't look dry and start peeling. I don't like it when my lips start peeling because I have to pull off the dead skin on my lips and sometimes it hurts because I peels off too much.

I also have to put lotion on my body, feet and face so that it won't look ashy especially around the mouth because of the toothpaste ring thing.

My mommy is always talking about how important it is to have good "hygiene", so she makes sure that me, my twin brother Zylee and my two younger siblings practice having good hygiene by checking our morning and night "To- Do" hygiene list every day.

Almost every morning my mom comes to my room and says the same thing: "Zolie, did you check off your hygiene 'To-Do' list for the morning??"

Then I say, "Yes, mommy, I did!!!"

But today my mom actually walked up to look at my hygiene list and said, "Zolie, you still have not changed the way you spell "Hi-Jean." I told you how to spell it, 'H-Y-G-I-E-N-E'."

Then I said, "I know mommy, but I spelled it that way so that I can remember how to say it right. Plus, I like how I drew my picture beside it, it's super cute!!"

She just looked at me and said, "Ok, Zolie, as long as you know that it is spelled wrong and by the way, I think the way you drew yourself is cute too." And then she smiled and walked out of my room to get my younger siblings up and ready for school too.

Do you want to know something cool? I like to wear little girl perfume because my mommy wears perfume for ladies and it smells so good.

My twin brother Zylee likes to wear little boy cologne because my dadcy wears cologne for men and because it smells so good. We like to be like our mommy and daddy especially when it comes to having good hygiene.

Guess what? My mom brought us our own bottles of smell good stuff. She got little girl perfume for me and little boy cologne for Zylee. She lets us do two sprays on the clothes that we are wearing and one spray on each wrist and we love it!! We love to smell good!! Do you like to smell good??

Well, since I am on the subject of smelling good, would you like to see my Hygiene list? Ok, here it is:

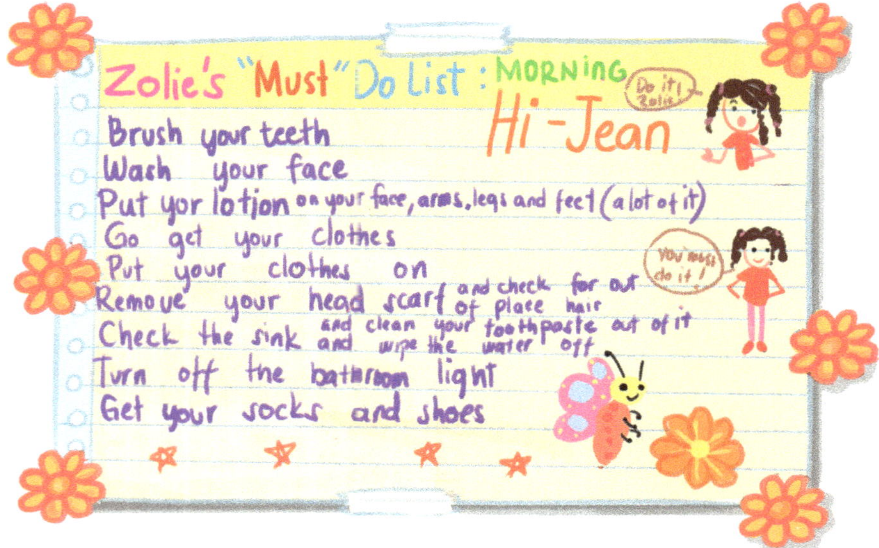

<u>Zolie's Morning *Hygiene "MUST" Do* List:</u>

- Brush your teeth
- Wash your face
- Put your lotion on your face, arms, legs, and feet (a lot of it)
- Put your chapstick on your lips
- Go get your clothes
- Put your clothes on
- Remove your head scarf and check for out of place hair
- Check the sink & clean your toothpaste out of it and wipe the water off
- Turn off the bathroom light
- Get your socks and shoes

What I like about getting ready in the morning is that we don't have to take baths because we take baths at night. So, for those of you who don't like taking baths don't get too excited because at this house we bathe and we have to do it every day.

My mom says that it takes up too much time and hot water for all of us to be taking baths in the morning so the children have to bathe at night.

We also have a list of "To-Dos" at night and it is a long list too. My mom said that B.O. is a no-no. The letters B and O are short for "Body Odor" which is a stinky smell that comes from your body when you have not cleaned it.

And do you want to know what else my mom says? She says, "Zolie, hygiene is very important and if you can't smell yourself then something is wrong with your nose. You should always practice good hygiene."

And then I usually say, "Mommy, don't worry, my nose is working just fine and I will practice good hygiene. I promise!!"

She usually just laughs at me and says, "Zolie Nova, you are something else princess!!" And then I say, "I know!!!"

Then we both laugh!! I love my mommy!!!

Oh, and as you can see, I am practicing good hygiene and so is Zylee ... so we think ...

Chapter 2

A'Lytha "Kipper"

Guess what?? Today I'm super-duper excited for two reasons. One is getting to play outside until it gets late because it's Friday and two is because my favorite cousin A'Lytha is coming down to spend the summer with us.

My cousin A'Lytha is nine years old and she is in the fifth grade. A'Lytha is very smart and she knows a whole lot of cool stuff. I always learn something new when she comes to stay during the summer. She is my favorite cousin in the whole wide world. I feel like we are sisters sometimes because she knows me so well and because we have so much in common.

A few summers ago Zylee and I gave her the nickname "Kipper" and she loves it and now everybody calls her Kipper, even her mom!! We call her Kipper because she likes to skip around all the time and because she is always happy. She has a funny laugh and is always laughing and smiling.

Do you want to know what else is funny about Kipper? She loves to eat and I mean really, really loves to eat.

Whenever you mention food she gets sooooo excited and starts dancing. And guess what? She doesn't like for you to take her plate of food up from the table until all of her food is gone and I do mean all of her food, including the crumbs. Yes, I said the crumbs!!

One of the things that Kipper and I have in common is playing outside. We like to play outside a lot and when I say a lot I mean from sunrise to sunset.

My mom usually gives me a full day of outdoor play time on the weekends if I have finished my homework from school and if I have completed my daily chores without having to be reminded. Kipper has chores too, but not as much as I do because she doesn't have her own room. Kipper sleeps in my room on my pullout bed or sometimes she falls asleep in the family room.

My chores change sometimes if it is laundry week because I have to sort out my own clothes. My mom taught me to sort my own clothes because she said if I can pick out my own clothes to wear to school, then I can sort out my own clothes to wash. My mom normally washes my clothes, but I know how to too.

Would you like to see my list of chores? Ok, here it is!

<u>Zolie's Chore List:</u>

- Fix your bed
- Open your blinds to let the sun in
- Sweep your floor*
- Clean under your bed*

- Dust your room*
- Empty your trash can*
- Clean your bathroom (wipe sink, clean out tub, sweep floor, empty trash)
- Check the kitchen and living room if it is your week to clean either one of them

  (The * sign means twice a week or as needed)

Kipper and I try to wake up real early on Saturday mornings so that we can do our part of the chores and have more time to play outside.

We are usually finished with all of our chores by 11 a.m. and this gives us plenty of time to go outside and play with our friends.

Kipper has friends out here too. She has a friend named Maluum (pronounced "May-lum") who lives down the street. Maluum is nine years old and she is really funny, she is always telling jokes. Kipper and Maluum became friends a few summers back when Kipper first came down from California.

We usually walk to Maluum's house to see if she can play and if she can then we walk down to the park

and meet up with Yoki, Messiah and other neigh-
borhood kids.

When all of us get together at the park, we like to start off by playing Double-Dutch to get our energy going. Double-Dutch is when we jump with two ropes, and two people can even jump together inside of both ropes. It is so fun!

We also play other fun games like Mother May I, Red light/Green light, Simon Says, hide and seek, and duck- duck, goose. We also like to ride on our bikes, skateboards and play other games like jacks and pixie sticks. Sometimes we even make mud pies with water and dirt.

One of my absolute favorite games to play is Tetherball. I always win when we play Tetherball, but sometimes it makes my hand hurt because you have to hit the ball hard and make it wrap around the pole.

As you can see, we love to play outside. Do you and your friends like playing outside?

My mom says that kids need to use their imagination more. She limits our time to watch t.v. so that we can read more. And if we do get to watch t.v., it is adult approved cartoons, something educational, or a kid friendly movie.

My mom says that electronics are taking us kids away from things that kids should be doing, like going outside to play, reading a book, coloring, playing dolls, board games, or other cool stuff for kids. She said that when she was a kid they didn't have all of this electronic stuff so they had a chance to enjoy their childhood and she wants us to do the same. Let kids be kids, is what she always says!!!

Well, back to me, Kipper, and our friends. Guess what else we decided to do today?? We decided to make a new cheer!! Do you want to hear it? Ok, here it goes:

"P- L- A- Y all my friends we PLAY outside

We playing yeah yeah we playing..

P- L- A- Y all my friends we PLAY outside

We playing yeah yeah we playing..

We like to skate yeahh we got them skates we got them skates
We like to swing yeahh we like to swing we like to swing to swing
We like to jump rope.. yeahh we play double dutch
Those are the things that you do when you're play-
ing with your crew..ayeee

P- L- A- Y all my friends we PLAY outside

We playing yeah yeah we playing.."

I just love making up cheers, it is so fun!!!

Do you and your friends play fun games that you make up? You should!! Or if you want to, you can play some of the games that me and my friends make up and play.

We had so much fun today and we even beat the street light before it came on too!!!! My mom says that we need to be home before the street light comes on.

My mom says that is not safe for children to play outside after the street light comes on because it means that it is about to get dark outside.

We had so much fun today!! I can't wait until to-morrow so that we can play all day again!!!!

Chapter 3

You don't smell that (my new smell)

So, we made it home on time and my mom and dad are in the kitchen cooking dinner and it smells so good. We are having nachos tonight and I am so happy and of course Kipper is super excited and so is Zylee.

My mom tells us to go and wash our hands so that we can get ready to eat dinner and before we can even say "Ok," Kipper was already coming out of the restroom from washing her hands. I looked up at Kipper and said, "Wow, Kipper, you washed your hands really fast!" Then Kipper replied, "Well, you know I love my food Zolie and I already knew what to do before Aunt Sandy could even say it!!"

I looked at her and said, "Well, I love food too, especially nachos," and then I rushed past her and hurried into the restroom alongside my siblings Zylee, Sahsha, and Sire.

As soon as the rest of us finished washing our hands, we all walked back into the kitchen to grab our plates to eat. I walked over to my mom and stood next to her to get my chips and she blurts out, holding her nose, "Somebody smells like strong onions and tangy tarts and all of you smell like outdoors."

And I replied, "Maybe it's just the nachos. Did you chop up onions in the meat for the nachos?"

Then my mom replied, "I didn't put onions in the nachos this time. And then I shrugged my shoulders and yelled out, "Well, it's not me …"

"Me either," Kipper said loudly and then Zylee says, "I don't smell onions, but I do smell those nachos … mmmm … I am so hungry, can we eat now?"

And then my mom says, "One of yall is cutting up, (meaning: "smelling real bad") and if you can't smell yourself then something is wrong with your nose."

And then she continued saying, "All of you need to go and take baths as soon as you finish eating dinner because that onion smell is really strong."

We all replied, "Yes ma'am" as we walked to the kids' table with our plate of nachos.

As we are eating, Kipper looks at me and sniffs near my arms and says, "Zolie, that onion tart smell is coming from you."

Then I say, "Nu-uh, no it's not." Kipper replied, "Yes it is, and you need to sniff under your arms."

And so I turned and sniffed under my arms and said, "I don't smell anything." Then I even put my finger under my arm and smelled it and pointed it towards Kipper saying, "See, I don't smell anything ..."

And then Kipper says, "Zolie, I almost choked on my food! Why did you just stick your finger under your armpit while you are eating? That is nasty! The first thing you need to do right now is wash your stinky finger before you finish eating and second, you need to get your nose checked because that smell is coming from under your armpits."

I replied, "Kipper, you need to get your nose checked because I don't smell anything, so it must be you."

"Um no, Zolie, it is not me because I wear deodorant," Kipper replied.

I looked at her and said, "Deoda-what?" And then Kipper said, "Deo-dorant. And then I said, "I don't even know what that is."

Kipper looks at me and says, "So, you obviously don't wear deodorant, well it is time that you do. Deodorant is what you use to keep your armpits from stinking when you sweat."

Then I said, "Well, I have never used deodorant before and I don't even know what it looks like. Mommy never told me that I needed it before."

And then Kipper says, "I know and that is because you didn't need it before, but now you do. I will show you mine," and before Kipper could go on talking, my mom interrupts us as she walks towards the kids' table and says, "Kipper, I heard y'all talking and before we suggest deodorant as a solution, let Zolie take a bath first and then I can decide what I need to do next. Thank you for wanting to teach her about deodorant, that is really sweet of you. We will know for sure between tonight and tomorrow morning if Zolie needs the 'deodorant talk' or not."

"Ok", replied Kipper.

I looked at my mom and said, "But what is that? What does deodorant look like?"

Then my mom says, "Well, first let's not talk hygiene at the table and second let's do what I suggested about the bath and we will discuss this later."

We all replied, "Yes ma'am" and turned to finish eating our food.

We were all quiet at the table after that talk and I still don't believe that my underarms stink. I can't smell it, it's not me.

After dinner we looked on the "chore chart" to see whose turn it was to do the dishes tonight and we see that it is Zylee's day, so Kipper and I go to the different bathrooms to prepare our bath water for our baths.

We have three bathrooms in our house: One for the boys, Zylee and Sire, one for the girls, me and Sahsha, and one for mommy and daddy. Oh, and we also have a bathroom for guests.

As we get out our pajamas in the room while waiting for our bathtubs to fill up with water, Kipper says, "Zolie, there are ways that you should know about to help you smell yourself." And then I say, "But Kipper, I don't stink! Do you see that hygiene chart over there?"

Kipper replied, "Yeah, I see it." Then I continued, saying, "Well, every day I have to check that hygiene chart off and I didn't miss anything today. Everything is checked off on the list."

And then Kipper interrupts me and says, "I know, Zolie, but we did play outside today and deodorant is not on your hygiene list."

Then I replied, "I know that it's not, so that must mean that I don't need it and besides, I don't even know what it is."

And then Kipper says, "Well, Aunt Sandy is about to teach you just like my mom had to teach me because I didn't know either. I didn't smell myself at first, but now I do all of the time because you should smell yourself before anyone else does."

And then I say, "Well, I do smell myself and I don't smell anything so I am just going to take a bath and then we shall see if I stink."

Then Kipper says, "Ok Zolie, but you do know that bathing is meant to take away the stink so you won't stink once you finish taking a bath, but we shall see between tonight and tomorrow if that smell comes back like Aunt Sandy said."

And then I looked at Kipper and shrugged my shoulders and we both went in separate directions to take our baths. Kipper goes to Zylee's bathroom to take her bath and I use my bathroom to take my bath.

After taking our baths we both smelled so good. I mean, we had my room smelling like soap and smell good lotion. I just knew that I didn't stink now so before Kipper could start talking to me I ran to my mommy's room.

I walked in saying, "Mommy, smell me. Mommy, do you still smell onions? Mommy, smell my arms," and then I stretch out my arms as I hugged her.

And then she said, "No, pumpkin, I don't."
Then I said, "See, I told you that it wasn't me. I smell good!!!"

And then she says, "Yes, you do for now, but we shall see what tomorrow brings because if it is your underarms then we will have to get that smell under control."

I replied, "Don't worry mommy, you won't be smelling onions again."

My mom says, "Ok my love bug, go ahead and get ready for bed. Make sure you do your 30 minutes of reading and make sure that the tub is cleaned out for Sahsha to get her bath."

Then I say, "Ok mommy, good night!!" And then I left her room.

When I got back to my room I couldn't wait to tell Kipper that my mom said that I didn't stink, so I knew it wasn't me. But as soon as I looked at her bed I saw that she had fallen asleep with her book in her hand. I was like, "Wow, she fell asleep fast," and then I looked at the purple tube that she had beside her and it said "Princess Tween D-E-O-D-O-R-A-N-T" on the label and it had a lid on it.

I stared at the purple tube before I took it from beside her to open it because I didn't want to wake her up, but since she was snoring I knew that she would be hard to wake up and besides, she did say that I needed to use it, but how? So, I just opened it up and smelled it and was like "hey, this smells good, I wonder if you can use this like you use perfume." But before I could think of the ways to use it I hurried and put the cap back on it and took it and sat it on the dresser because I remembered something that my mommy said about messing with other people's belongings. She said that you don't take what is not yours without permission because that is considered stealing so I just left the purple tube alone and decided to wait to the morning to ask Kipper about it.

Today was a long day and I am really sleepy now. I will talk to you in the morning. I have to finish up all of my last-minute stuff!! Good night!!!

 # Chapter 4 

That Smell Again

So, it's a new day and as always my alarm clock wakes me up at 6:10 a.m., I like my alarm clock it is pretty cool, it is shaped like a butterfly. Do you have an alarm clock to wake you up?

I have to be ready by 7:15 a.m. and I have to have my chore list checked off before I can leave the house. I looked at my clock and it was already 6:20 am, so I jump out of my bed, fixed my bed and then I head to the restroom to start my daily routine.

While rushing to the restroom, I stopped to look at the purple tube of deodorant sitting on the dresser and I sniffed my armpits and said to myself, "I still don't smell anything, so I guess I want be needing deodorant today or anytime soon."

I turned and looked over at Kipper who was still sleeping and thought to myself, "See, I told you so, ha-ha."

As soon as I get to the restroom I turned on the water and began brushing my teeth and washing my face. After washing my face I put on lotion and then I squeeze more out to put some on my body too because my mom says that my arms shouldn't look like I dipped them in powdered sugar.

The next thing I do is make sure that I clean out the sink, being sure to clean out any clumps of toothpaste left inside of it, because my mom says nobody wants to see what you spit out of your mouth, Zolie. And believe me, I know what she means because it does look gross when I look into the sink and see clunks of toothpaste that someone else spit inside of it or around it.

As I rushed back to my room to put my clothes on, my mom walks in and says, "Zolie, is my black comb in your barrette box?"

And then I say, "I don't know, let me look." And then I go to the dresser to get out my barrette box to look and as I am looking, my mom says, "Uh-uh Zolie, no ma'am, no ma'am." And then I say, "What mommy?"

Then she says, "Zolie, I smell that smell again."

Then I replied, "The strong musty onion
tart smell?"

Then she says, "Yes Zolie, and it is you," and then I
say, "But, mommy, no, it is not me ... I don't smell
it ... maybe it's Kipper."

And my mom said, "Zolie, it is not Kipper because
her arms are under the covers. Did you wash under your armpits last night Zolie? And I said, "Yes
ma'am, I did, I just washed my arms like I normally
do." And then she said, "You couldn't have washed

under your armpits, Zolie, because you smell the same way as last night, just not as strong."

And then I just said, "But mommy, I came to let you smell me last night and you said that I smelled good."

Then she replied, "That was last night after your bath Zolie and you have slept since then. Sometimes you can sweat when you sleep and it smells like you must have sweated in your sleep and that is why the onion tart smell is back."

"I'm sorry, mommy." I said. "I will scrub under my armpits tonight when I take a bath again." And then my mom shook her head and said, "Sorry won't stop that body odor happening right now Zolie, and on top of that you don't smell it so something must be wrong with your nose."

And then she looked at her watch and continued by saying, "We don't have enough time for you to take another bath right now because we are already in a rush this morning, but you will need to go and wash under those armpits again with soap."

Pouting, I turned to her and said, "But I don't smell anything mommy. It's not as strong as you think it is, I did everything on the hygiene list today except for put on my perfume which I am about to do now."

And then my mom says, "Zolie, don't put that perfume on top of that smell."

And then I say, "But mommy, it is under my arms that you say I stink, not my wrist. Please can I put it on?" Normally we get into big trouble for pouting and back talking, but this time she said, " You know what Zolie, I don't have time to address this like I want to at this moment so go ahead and put it on if you want to; you are just adding sweet to a sour smell."

And then she added, "And since it is not you, I guess you will have to go to school smelling just like musty onions today and I want you to tell me just how many of your classmates tell you how good you smell today since you say that every day in your first period of class some of your classmates always scoot up next to you and say 'mmm you smell so good Zolie,' I want to know what they will say today."

And then I said, "Ok."

Then my mom continues more by saying, "Well, today you will find out who your friends are because your real friends will tell you if you stink. Today, and today alone, will be the ONLY day that I will allow you to go to school smelling like this, do you understand? You are a reflection of me Zolie Zi, and I will not allow you to make me or yourself look bad, but today I will let you learn this lesson the hard way since you don't want to listen to me and also because something is obviously wrong with your nose. I will talk to you about deodorant this evening when you get home from school since you don't think your underarms stink. You will have to start using deodorant from now on. Go ahead and grab your stuff and let's go. Don't worry about the comb, we have lost time having to stop and talk about your hygiene this morning."

And then I grabbed my backpack and followed my mom who was walking towards Zylee's room to make sure he was ready to go.

As she approaches Zylee's room, Zylee comes to the door and then she looks down at his feet and says, "Zylee, I hope that you remembered to put on some fresh socks today because I have been noticing that stinky sock smell coming from your laundry basket again."

And then Zylee replied, "Huh? What smell, mom?"

My mom replies, "You know that 'dill pickle' smell like someone is pickling your feet? Well, the only

time that smell happens is when you don't change
your socks, Zylee. I do not want to be touching stiff
socks that smell like dill pickles when I am putting
your clothes in the washing machine. You should
not be wearing stiff stinky dirty socks, Zylee Zi.
You need to make sure that you put dirty socks in
the dirty clothes basket and not back on your feet. I
don't understand why you don't notice the smell or
how stiff they are when you are putting your socks
on your clean feet. It makes no sense to me."

And then Zylee replies, "Mom, I promise you, I
have on clean socks today. I promise you." And then
she says, "Ok Zylee, clean socks mean clean smelling shoes ... dirty socks mean dirty smelling shoes
... do you understand?"

"Yes, ma'am", replied Zylee and then he looks at me
and says, "Good morning, Zolie."

Then I say, "Good morning, brother," and then we
smile. We are always smiling and laughing. I love
having a twin brother.

After that, we all rushed to the car and head to the bus stop so that Zylee and I can get to school on time.

Chapter 5

The Bus Ride

So, we are waiting for the school bus to arrive and it finally does about ten minutes after my mom left. We don't have assigned seats on the bus so Messiah normally saves me a seat next to her.

Once the bus pulls up, I get on the bus and see that Messiah is waving at me so that I can sit next to her. I walked over to her and sat down next to her and waved and said, "Good morning friend," and then I put my backpack in front of me.

She suddenly puts her hand over her nose and mouth and says, "Good morning Zolie," and then she coughs saying, "Hold up …"

Then I say, "Are you all right, Messiah?" And Messiah, who is still holding her hand over her nose and mouth, says, "Girl, I lost my breath for a minute," and then I say, "What? You lost your breath?" and then she says, "Yeah," and then she continues by saying, "Zolie, please don't wave your arm like that anymore …"

Then I replied, "What? Why?" And she said, "Because I smelled something that made my nose tingle, something that smelled like soggy socks or some strong onions and it came from your direction when you waved."

And then I said, "Well, I don't know what it could've been," and then she says, "Well, I do because I have smelled it before and so have you."

 I looked at her with a frown and said, "Where? Where have I smelled it before?"

Messiah just looked at me and said, "Two words: Carmen Michaels." And then with my mouth hanging open I repeated, "CARMEN Michaels?? No way, I don't smell that bad." Messiah just coughed and said, "Almost worse."

And then she got up to crack open the window on the bus and asked "Do you wear deodorant yet?"

"No," I said. "I don't even know what that is. I saw Kipper's last night and the only reason that I knew that it was deodorant was because it was spelled out on the tube."

Then Messiah said, "Well, I do and I had to start wearing it when I was six years old because my underarms smelled like yours do now. It took me almost two weeks to finally pick up the smell because I didn't smell it either."

"Ugghhhh," I replied. "I wish that everybody would stop telling me that my underarms smell. I don't smell anything."

Messiah said, "Well, you might want to start sniffing harder because everyone at school will smell you every day if you don't get this under control and why are you getting so upset, Zolie? I am just telling you that you have a smell coming from you that is not your usual smell, good perfume smell. It smells like your perfume mixed with onions and soggy socks."

Then I said, "Well, my mom, Kipper, and Zylee said the same thing last night and this morning too, but I don't smell anything at all and I don't know what to do about something that I can't smell. It is like y'all want me to imagine a smell that is not there."

Messiah replied, "Ohhh, but it is there Zolie and it wants the world to know about it. Why didn't your mom just go ahead and have you put on deodorant before you left home today?"

With an irritated voice I answered, "Because I told her that I didn't stink so she said 'Ok, go to school smelling just like that and see what happens. And now I wish I would've just asked her to please let me put on the deodorant or at least wash up under my arms."

At this point I just dropped my head down to stare at the floor of the bus and said, "I can see this is going to be a long day. Thanks Messiah. Ughhhhh."

Messiah just looked at me and said, "Well, I'm sorry if I hurt your feelings, Zolie, but hey, look at the bright side of it, at least your mom didn't do to you what my mom did to me. My mom got so upset that I didn't smell myself that she just yelled at me and said, 'Do you want me to smack your face off?!! How come you don't smell that, that is unacceptable, Messiah!!' and then I said, No, I don't want you to smack my face off mom and then she said, 'Well, you had better figure out a way to smell yourself when your underarms stink. You should be able to smell yourself since you are the only one who is with you all the time.' And then she said, 'I am going to teach you how to use deodorant and you better not forget to put it on as long as you have under arm pits.'"

And then Messiah continued with a scared look on her face saying, "Zolie, I had to start sniffing my underarms really hard from the time I took baths to the time I got up to see if I smelled different from the way I did when I took a bath and it took me a couple of weeks, but I finally smelled it one day and now if I smell that smell coming on me after recess or gym class I hurry and go wash under my armpits with soap and put my deodorant on again. I also sniff my shirt under the armpits to make sure I am not stinky too and it helps. I finally got it.

I just looked at her and said, "Wow, that is horrible, Messiah. It sounds like you had a hard time, just like me. Well, my mom just said that something must be wrong with my nose because I can't smell myself. I mean, I smell my breath because she told me how too, but I don't smell my armpits at all. I even wash under my nails when I wash my hands to make sure that they are extra clean,but I guess that bad hygiene can happen anywhere on your body."

And then I continued and said, "I hope that my mom doesn't have to smack my face off though because then I won't be able to smell myself at all if I don't have a face and a nose to sniff from! I don't know what to do and now I don't want to go to school since everyone can smell me but me."

Messiah just looked at me and said, "Well, Zolie, the only thing that I can suggest you do is to stop by the restroom to wash under your armpits when you get to school and to keep your arms down all day and try not to stand close to too many people because if you do, someone is going to smell you. Also, try to start sniffing your shirt under the armpits really hard just to see if you smell anything weird. Try to start noticing how your shirt smells before you put it on and after you take it off at night."

And then I said, "Ok, I will try that. I hope
that I finally smell myself. This is not good, not
good at all."

And then Messiah says, "I know. I have been in your
shoes before." And then I just sighed.

After that we rode in silence until we got to school
because I didn't want to talk anymore because I felt
bad that everyone smells me but me. I mean, why
can't I smell myself? Maybe something is wrong
with my nose.

Chapter 6

School Blues

So, we arrive at school and all of the kids are getting off the bus and I decided to wait to be the last student to get off of the bus. As we are walking towards the school building to go inside, Messiah whispers to me, "Don't forget to keep your arms down, Zolie," and then I say, "Umm, ok" and then we go our separate ways to go to our classroom.

Since I already know that my underarms stink, I really don't want to go to class so I go straight to the restroom like Messiah told me to do so that I can wash under my armpits with some soap. And can you believe this? They ran out of soap, so that means that I can't wash under my armpits. What am I going to do now??

I don't have enough time to go to the other side of the school to go to the other restroom to see if they have soap. Well, I guess this means that I have no choice but to go to class with stinky armpits. I guess that I just have to sit there and be embarrassed about a smell that I can't smell. I guess that I will just stink everybody out of the classroom and then everybody will be mad at me for causing a stinking mess. Now I really don't want to go to class.

As soon as I turned to look at the door, I started to see lots of students walking past the restroom heading to class and then one girl named Kiye walked in and said, "Oh, hey Zolie, I didn't see you standing there," and then I said, "Hey Kiye, I was just leaving."

And then I got really nervous because what if she smelled me? What if she thinks I stink? I lifted up my armpits once more and sniffed really hard just to see if I smelled something different, but I still don't.

I am so scared to go to class now because I can't smell myself and now everyone else will smell me. My mind starts to race again and I started thinking, what if I get told that I smell like Carmen Michaels and get bullied because I stink?

My classmates always say that Carmen smells like hot garbage and onions. I feel bad for saying this, but she really does smell like that and even worse when it's hot outside. I wonder if she can smell herself. I wonder if anyone has ever told her that she stinks. She has one friend named Manda, but they say Manda stinks too, so I don't know. Maybe something is wrong with their noses like something is wrong with mine.

Well, just in case you were wondering, I never join in on bullying them or calling them names. I always tell the teacher that they are being bullied. Bullying is not nice. I should know since I have been bullied before.

And right before I could think anymore scarifying thoughts the school bell rang and that meant I had to get to class or get into big trouble which could mean after school detention because students are not allowed to roam the school halls without a hall pass.

When the school bell rang I saw kids hurrying to their classroom doors where the teacher is standing there waiting for the last kid to come in so that they can close the door. I wasn't too far from Ms. Mahogany's classroom, but I tried to wait so that I could be the very last kid to go into the classroom door. Luckily, I was and I walked up just as Ms. Mahogany was about to shut the door.

I hurried past her with my armpits down and said, "Hi, Mrs. Mahogany," and rushed towards my seat.

Mrs. Mahogany usually gives us about seven minutes to get settled while she writes a daily phrase on the chalk board and gets settled at her desk.

Believe it or not, every morning some of my classmates scoot their chairs next to me in the group huddle and say, "Umm Zolie, you smell so good," and then I say, "I know and thank you!! But today is different. I don't smell so good so I am hoping that today no one scoots up next to me during group huddle.

However, that was not the case, as soon as I took my seat by Ms. Mahogany's desk, this boy named Nixon says, "Hey, there she is! Hey, Zolie, girl you were the last one in class today, that's not like you," and then before I could say anything back to him I suddenly hear my classmates' chairs scooting up next to me.

And then I thought, "Oh nooo!" ... And not even a second later I start to hear my classmates sniff-

49

ing the air and then one them says, "Ewww, Zolie, what is that new smell? I don't like that perfume." Then another one says, "Eww, Zolie, you smell like onions," and then another one says, "Zolie, did you forget to take a bath today?" And then all of a sudden I could hear all of the chairs scoot away from me and then I just put my head down and sigh ... I didn't say anything.

Nixon turned around in his chair and says, "Psst, Zolie, what happened girl? You usually smell so good." And then I say, "Nothing happened," and then he says, "Something happened, Zolie ... something happened girl." I just looked away in an attempt to ignore Nixon and before I could say anything else Mrs. Mahogany stands up at the chalkboard and says, "Good morning, class," and then she asks all of us to take our seats because we will not be having our morning huddle today.

I was happy that we were not having our morning huddle today because that meant that I didn't have to sit there and make everyone's nose hair tingle because of my bad hygiene.

This is going to be a long day. I can't smell myself.
Everybody smells me, but me. I just want to go
home. I wish I was home.

51

Chapter 7

A Conversation with Carmen

The school day seems to be dragging, but I have gotten through most of the day by avoiding raising my arms and avoiding people in every way possible by slowly moving away if someone is closer to me and by pretending that I don't hear someone talking to me so that I don't have to answer.

I know that sounds horrible, but I just don't want to hear that I stink anymore today. I even asked Messiah to leave me alone for the day too.

And as crazy as it sounds, during recess, I decided to walk over to Carmen Michaels and talk to her because I knew that she wouldn't say that I stink. I wondered if she would smell my stinky underarm pits and say anything about it. And guess what? She didn't.

So, I decided to ask Carmen if she could smell anything different about me today and she said, "Well, now that you ask me, I do smell some onions but I just figured it was something that you ate at lunch time Zolie."

Then she said, "Why are you asking me that Zolie?" And I said, "Well, you wouldn't understand." And then she said, "Try me and you just might see that I do understand."

"Well," I explained, "people have been telling me all day that my underarms stink and that I smell really bad today, so I have just been avoiding people all day because to be honest I can't even smell myself, but I guess everyone else can."

Then Carmen replied, "Zolie, people say that about me every day. I am so used to hearing people say that I stink and how bad I smell that it doesn't even bother me anymore."

And then I said, "But Carmen, don't you smell yourself?"

"Sometimes I do." she replied and she continued, saying, "but most times I don't because I am so used to it now."

I interrupted her saying, "But how can you be used to it, Carmen?"

Then Carmen said, "See, what most people don't know is that I am homeless, Zolie. I have no home. My family and I live on the streets and we sleep in shelters when they have rooms available for us to sleep in, but we sleep in my mom's car most of the time. See, my mom was laid off from her job almost two years ago and she has had a hard time trying to find a good job so she works different temp jobs to at least keep gas in her car so that we can move around. I wear dirty clothes all the time because we barely have enough money to even eat sometimes, so washing clothes isn't normally on the list, so we just wash when we can."

I sat in disbelief as I listened to Carmen. I couldn't believe what I was hearing. My eyes got really big and tears started to fill them and then I couldn't hold it any longer and I began to cry. I tried to stop, but I couldn't stop.

Then Carmen said, "Don't cry Zolie, it's ok. I guess that my life is supposed to be like this for some reason."

With tears streaming down my cheeks I replied, "No one deserves to live like that Carmen, no one."

And then I asked, "How come you haven't told anyone up here at the school so that you can get some help?"

Carmen just looked at me and sighed with tears in her eyes and said, "Because my mom says that I can't tell anyone at the school, so I don't say anything at all because I am afraid. I don't know what they would do if they found out that I was homeless."

Then I replied, "I am so sorry, Carmen. I am so sorry for judging you and for not taking the time to come and talk to you before."

And then Carmen looked at me saying, "It's ok, Zolie. I am used to people judging me and it just doesn't bother me anymore. I imagine that I am invisible most of the time." And then she just laughed and said, "Funny huh?"

Then I said, "Not really, Carmen. Sorry."

There were a few seconds of silence between us and then I looked at her and said, "I am going to help you Carmen. I promise."

And then Carmen said, "I have heard that before from people we meet on the streets and I thank you, but the only thing that I ask is that you don't tell the school. And please don't tell any of our class-mates either. Manda and you are the only ones that know this and that is all who needs to know."

Then I replied, "I won't. I promise. I want to see if my mom will allow me to use some of my allowance to give to you so that you can give it to your mom to wash your school clothes and maybe we can even buy you some washing detergent too. I am sure that we could. I will even ask about getting some extra food for you too."

Carmen replied, "That sounds really nice Zolie."

Then I said, "If I got you some deodorant and some hygiene stuff, would you use it?"

Carmen replied, "Of course I would." And then I said, "Ok, let me talk to my mom about it and let me learn how to use deodorant tonight when my mom teaches me and then I will teach you. Togeth-er, we will learn how to have good hygiene again. Together, we can do it."

And then Carmen said, "Thank you Zolie. I definitely need a friend like you right now and I hope that one day I can return the favor by being a good friend to you too."

Then I said, "Carmen, you have taught me a good lesson today and that is to not judge a person because you don't know how hard their life may be. We are just kids and life shouldn't be so hard for us. Thank you for sharing your life story with me today."

And then right when Carmen was about to say something else, the school bell rang for us to line up and go back to our classrooms.

I quickly grabbed Carmen's hand and said, "Come on, Carmen, we had better hurry to get in line before we get left outside," and then Carmen looked at me and smiled and said, "Ok, let's run!"

And we begin to run down the hill to join the other students lining up to go to their classes. Carmen and I go to different classes after lunch so I had to let go of her hand and waved at her and said, "Carmen, you are all right with me. I can't wait to see you tomorrow. See ya my friend!!"

And then Carmen waved back at me and said, "Zolie, you give me hope!! See you tomorrow!!"

As I stood in line looking at Carmen as she ran to join the other students in her class I thought to myself, "Wow, I thought that my day was really bad, but it really isn't."

I am even more determined to smell myself now so that I can teach Carmen how to smell herself so that she can have better hygiene and even make some new friends. I can't wait to get home to tell my mom about Carmen and I can't wait to learn how to put on deodorant when I get home.

Today wasn't so bad after all.

Chapter 8

Finally Home

The school day has finally ended and I am on the school bus heading home. I decided to sit by myself on the ride home because I wanted to think about what Carmen and I had talked about at recess.

When we finally got to my stop, I rushed off the bus and ran ahead of Zylee to get home very fast because I wanted to hurry up and learn how to smell myself. I wanted to see what my mom would say about Carmen. And I wanted to go into my piggy bank to see just how much money I could give to help Carmen and her mom.

As soon as I walked into the house, I yelled, "Zolie's in the house!" but I didn't see my mom anywhere nor did I see Kipper so I started yelling out, "Mommy, mommy, where are you? Mommy, I need to talk to you."

My mother came out from the kitchen where she was preparing food for dinner and said," Hey Zolie,

is everything ok? And why are you so out of breath?
How was school today?"

"Good," I said, "and bad, but more good than bad,
but ..." And just as I was about to say something
else, Kipper walks up from the family room and
says, "Hey, favorite cousin!!!" And then I looked at
her with a smile and waved saying, "Hey, Kipper!!"

And then Kipper made a weird face and said, "Uh-
oh, favorite cousin ... I smelled that tart onion
smell again when you waved," and before she could
continue I interrupted her and said, "I know, Kip-

per, you don't have to say it. Everyone at school told me how bad I smelled today. I know that I stink.

And with a smile Kipper said, "I wasn't trying to be mean. I just wanted you to know that it was back."

I replied, "I know, but I promise you, today will be the last day you smell that smell on me."

And then I turned around and said, "Mommy can I please talk to you alone."

And then she turned around and said, "Sure, Zolie. We can go into the family room where we can sit and talk."

Then I said "Ok."

I immediately turned back around and looked over at Kipper and said, "Sorry, Kipper, but I have to tell mommy something that I promised I wouldn't tell anyone else." And Kipper replied, "I understand Zolie. Talk to you in a few."

I said "Ok", and then my mom and I walked to the family room.

Once we got to the family room, I was really scared to tell my mom about Carmen being homeless because I didn't want her to tell the school or anyone else what I was about to tell her. I began to tell her the story about Carmen, but before I could start, I looked and her and said, "Mommy, before I tell you what I am about to tell you, you have to promise me by pinky promise that you will not tell anyone else, not even daddy."

My mom replied, "Well, Zolie, if it is something that your dad needs to know then I will have to tell him, but if it is not then I won't tell him."

"Ok," I said and then we shook hands with our pinkies.

Chapter 9

The Talk

"Ok", I said, "Now that you have promised not to tell I can begin. But, before I begin, you might want to sit down for this one because there is a lot to tell."

"Ok," she said with a laugh.

Then I said, "Let's start from the beginning. When the school day began it was horrible and I did have a stinking day at school because of my underarms. Everyone kept asking me, 'What happened, Zolie? Did you forget to take a bath today, Zolie? How come you can't smell yourself, Zolie Zi?' And I was really embarrassed because mom, I really didn't smell myself and I still don't smell myself."

Then my mom said, "Umm hmm ... see, I told you."

And then I continued, "You were also right when you said that I would find out who my friends were today and I did. Messiah was the first friend to tell me that I was stinky because she smelled me as soon as I sat next to her on the school bus and waved. She said that my smell took her breath away. And at first I was really upset with her because she didn't have to say it like that, but then she apologized and said that she went through the same thing that I am going through now where she couldn't smell herself.

And guess what Mom?"

"What", my mom said.

I said, "Her mom told her that she was going to smack her face off is she didn't learn to smell herself?"

And then my mom said, "Smack her face off? Oh my!" Then I said, "I know, I thought the same thing."

And then I looked my mom in the eyes and said, "Are you going to smack my face off if I don't smell myself? I mean, you wouldn't do that to me, would you?"

Then my mom said, "No, I wouldn't do that to you, but I am going to show you ways that you can smell yourself today so that you can recognize that smell before it gets out of control again."

Looking puzzled my mom added, "So, is this what you wanted to tell me? That Messiah's mom said that she was going to smack her face off?"

"No," I replied. "I am getting to that part." And she said, "Oh, ok."

Then I continued, "So as you know, today I didn't want to be around anyone because I was really tired of hearing people say that my underarms stink. I mean, who wants to hear that all day? I know I didn't. So, I decided to go and play with Carmen Michaels during recess because I was thinking, well since she stinks too, she won't complain about my stinky armpits."

And then my mom said with a surprised look on her face, "Are you talking about the Carmen Michaels that you said that all of your classmates call stinky?"

"Yes," I replied.

With a strange look on her face my mom said, "Now Zolie, I know you did not go bully her, or go try to act funny towards her so this better be nice."

Then I said, "Mommy, (as I slumped my shoulders down) no, I didn't go bully her, I don't bully other kids and you know that because of what happened to me when I was getting bullied by Charlene and Tonya."

Then she said, "Ok, Zolie, you can continue."

And I continued saying, "Mommy, I found out why Carmen stinks. I found out and it is horrible. Carmen is homeless, mommy and she lives out on the streets with her mother. She has to wear dirty clothes to school and she can't even take baths like normal kids take baths. She said she has no food sometimes. Sometimes they eat food that people throw out. It is so sad mommy I don't understand … she … she …"

And before I could finish telling the story, I was already crying very hard. My mom had to pull me to her and hug me to calm me down because I was very upset.

My mom said, "Zolie, calm down, Zolie, calm down. Look at me," she said.

And then I looked at her and said, "But why, mommy, why? This isn't fair? Why is this happening to her? What did she do wrong? Is she a bad person? I don't understand this mommy. Can we help her mommy? Can we help?"

Then my mom said, "Yes Zolie, but how did you get her to tell you all of this?"

I replied, "Well, because when I walked over to play with Carmen at recess I asked her if she could smell me and she said yes she could. And then I asked her if she could smell me, then why couldn't she smell herself? Then she told me that she was homeless and had been homeless for going on two years now. I didn't know what to say. I mean, I didn't understand how come she couldn't go to a home every day like me or other kids. I don't understand how this could be happening to a kid."

And then my mom replied, "Zolie, let me try to help you understand this. Unfortunately life is different for everyone. Not everyone lives in a home Zolie. In the grown-up world the adults have to get jobs in order to take care of their families and if they don't have a job, they can't take care of their family."

Then I said, "But no one should be sleeping outside in their car, and sometimes it rains and snows so where do they go? Sometimes it is really hot outside or really cold outside, so who helps them mommy?"

And then my mom said, "Well, sometimes people can get help and sometimes there is no help available so some families don't have a choice but to sleep outside."

And then I started crying again and said, "Aww that is horrible mommy, just horrible. Can they stay with us until they get a home? Can they?"

Then my mom replied, "Zolie, that is a very big decision to make and I would love to do that, but unfortunately we can't do that right now because we have a very full house with you, your three siblings, me, your dad and now Kipper."

And then I said, "But we have a family room. Can't they stay there?"

My mom replied, "No, but we can see how we can help them and we will help them as much as we can. The first thing that we have to do is find out whether her mother wants her family to be helped. Carmen will have to get permission from her mother in order for us to help her with the bigger stuff. Right now, we can help her with little stuff."

"Little stuff like what," I said.

And then my mother said, "Well, you can put a little hygiene bag together for Carmen to leave in her locker so that she can have some things to help her freshen up while she is at school.

And then I interrupt and say, "Ok, if her mom says yes we can help her, can we get her some little girl perfume too because we want her to smell really good?"

And then my mom replied, "Yes, we can."

Then I said with a smile, "This is awesome. I am so excited, mommy. Carmen said that people say that they will help her and never do. I am glad that we can help her."

My mom smiled and said, "We will do what we can for them and as much as we can for them, but if her mother is not happy with our help then we will not be able to do much more."

Then I said, "Yeah, Carmen said that she is afraid to get help because her mom told her not to tell anyone, especially the school."

My mom replied, "Exactly, Zolie!" Then she said, "Zolie, there are a lot of kids like Carmen in this world so you should consider yourself very lucky to have a home and food to eat every day."

And I replied, "Yes, very lucky," and then I hugged my mom.

She grabbed my hand and said, "Zolie, you continue to be a friend to Carmen by encouraging her and by being there for her, ok?"

And then I said, "Ok, I will. I hope that she doesn't have to live like this forever."

My mom said, "Nothing is forever, Zolie. As long as her mom is trying to make things better for them it will get better."

Then I said, "Can I take her a hygiene bag tomorrow? Can we go to the store for her stuff tonight? I can use my allowance money, I don't mind."

My mom smiled and replied, "Yes, but make sure her mom is ok with it going forward." And then I said, "Ok, I will."

Then my mom said, "Ok, well what needs to happen first is our talk about your hygiene because you can't help anybody if you can't help yourself."

I said, "You're right mommy and I want to
help myself!"

Then she hugged me and said, "I am so proud of you for taking responsibility for yourself and your hygiene. You really have a big heart by wanting to take responsibility to help someone else too. You never cease to amaze me Zolie Zi."

And then I say, "Thanks mom, I get it from you!!"
And then she hugs me again.

I am grateful for my mom. I am grateful for a home, food and clothes. I am grateful for everything!
Now, I am ready to learn about this deodorant.

 # Chapter 10 

So what is Deodorant?

After my mom and I finished talking and I finally understood the why's about Carmen, she began to talk to me about my hygiene and how I can help myself.

My mom starts off by saying, "Ok, Zolie, now that you understand about Carmen and her mom, let's head over to your room and talk about what we have going on in there. I have laid out your outfit from yesterday so that you can smell your clean shirts and dirty shirts to help you start to notice the change in smells under your arm pits."

Then I said, "Eww, sounds stinky already, but I really want to know the difference, so let's get started."

When we walked into my room, the first thing I say is, "Eww, it stinks in here. It smells like onions and something sour or soggy. Kipper got it stinky in here today."

Then my mom says, "No, it isn't Kipper, honey, it is all you. Kipper has been in the family room all day so that I can get this room ready for you. I closed all of your windows and turned off your air-freshener and closed the door so that your room can absorb the smell. I wanted you to smell this smell as soon as you opened the door to your room."

And I replied, "Whew, it is strong. Can we open the windows please?"

And then she replied, "No, not yet. I need you to understand that this is what everyone smells when they smell your armpits. Every area, and I do mean every area, of your body needs to be scrubbed. I need you to understand that from now on you will need to wear deodorant because your underarms smell like this room and if you don't like the smell in your room, then why would anyone else? I mean, would you want to stay in this room and smell it all day without being allowed to open your window to air your room out?"

And then I said, "No ma'am ... it smells horrible in here. Can we open the window now?"

She shook her head saying, "No, not yet. I need
you to pick up yesterday's shirt that you played in
and sniff the armpits and then you need to pick up
your nightgown and sniff the armpits. I need you to
recognize the difference in the smells. One smells
stronger in the stinky onion smell and the other
is not as strong but it is tart. And I want you to
tell me why."

And then I say, "Ok" and sniffed them both and
continue by saying, "Eww ... eww ... they both
smell so bad ... how come I didn't smell this?" And
then I held up the shirt while holding my nose
saying, "I guess this shirt smells the worse because

I played outside in it all day. I don't know why my nightgown smells just as bad, it kind of smells like a tangy sour tart of some sort."

My mom then replied holding up the gown saying, "Well, the gown smells bad because when you took your bath, you did not scrub under your arms, you just washed yourself like you normally do.

Then I said, "Oh, ok, but what makes my armpits smell so bad and how does deodorant help?"

My mom grabbed a pink tube of deodorant that was sitting on top of my dresser and said while pointing to the pink tube, "Do you see this tube? It is called deodorant and deodorant is a substance applied to the body to prevent body odor caused by the bacterial breakdown of sweat in armpits, feet, and other areas of the body.

And then I said, "Oh, ok." And then I pointed to the deodorant and said, "Is that my deodorant, mommy? Is that the one you got for me?

Then she replied, "Yes Zolie, it is.

And then I replied, "Yaay!! I am excited and I can't wait to use it. Can I see it, mommy? Can I hold it?"

And then she said, "Yes, and come here so that I can show you how to put it on."

I walked closer to her and she told me to lift up my arm and then she opened the pink tube that had white stuff inside of it and rubbed it up and down my armpits. And then I said, "Mommy, that tickles and it smells so good."

Then she said, "I know it smells good and your underarms and everyone else around you will thank you for using it. The more you use it, the less it will tickle you.”

And I replied, “Oh ok!” and then I sniffed my armpits and said, “but mommy, I still smell the onion tart smell a little.”

Then she replied, “Well, that is because you haven’t taken your bath and washed that smell away yet. I just wanted to show you how to use it now, but this is a good example for you to see how putting deodorant over stinky armpits still doesn’t stop the armpits from stinking, so you have to always take a bath before putting it on.”

And then I said, “Oh, ok,” and nodded my head because I was trying to remember everything so that I can tell Carmen at school tomorrow.

“Mommy,” I said, “I promise you that I will practice having better hygiene from now on. No more onion smells here, I don’t like feeling like everyone can smell my stinking arms all day long.”

Then my mom said, "Good! I am glad to hear that, Zolie. I knew that you would catch on very quickly."

I smiled and replied, "I had no choice!! I hope that Carmen will catch on as fast as I did. I want to help her smell good too!!"

And then my mom said, "Look at you, Zolie, you have such a thoughtful heart. "

I replied, "Thanks, mommy, and now can we get ready to go and get Carmen her hygiene stuff?"

My mom turned to me and said, "Yes, we can go after I finish your braiding your hair for school tomorrow!" We will have to grab something to eat for you while we are out.

Then I said, "Alright!!" And then I hugged my mom and said, "Thank you so much, mommy. I knew that I could come to you about Carmen and for my hygiene!! You are the best mom in the world!!!"

I love that I can tell my mom everything. I hope that you can tell your mom or care taker anything too. It really helps when you know that someone is there to listen.

 # Chapter 11 

Carmen again-Back to School

I am really excited today because for one, I put on my deodorant all by myself and two, I smell really good. Guess what I know, I know that everybody will scoot next to me in class and say, "Umm, Zolie, you smell sooo good," like they always do.

I am a little nervous though because I get to give Carmen all of the Hygiene stuff. I really hope that she likes it.

Do you want to know what we got her? Ok, here it is:

We got her some tubes toothpaste, a couple of deodorants, some toothbrushes and a case to hold her toothbrush, some dental floss, packages of six-pack soaps, some socks, some under shirts, some undergarments, a twelve-pack of little towels, six big towels, a comb, a brush, two shampoos and two conditioners, outfits, a new pair of shoes, laundry detergent and two duffle bags for her clean clothes and one for her dirty clothes. We also got stuff for her mom and her sister too.

We are also giving her the small Z-hygiene bag which is something she can leave at school that just has stuff in there like: deodorant, toothbrush, toothpaste, soap, a wash cloth, brush and comb.

Yeah, I know, we got her a lot of stuff, but yesterday when Carmen and I were talking, these were the things that she said she needed, including the shoes.

I didn't know that my mom and dad would get all of the stuff I asked them to, but they did and they even got her some headbands too. Well, I actually asked them if I could I use $60 of my saved allow-ance money to chip in to get her more stuff and they said that it was ok.

I can't give her all of her stuff until her mom says that it is ok, but I can give her the Z-Hygiene bag today because it is small and she can leave it at school.

My mom decided to drive me to school today be-cause we stayed out late last night shopping for

Carmen and because I had more stuff to carry besides my backpack and she didn't want me to have to carry all of that stuff on the school bus. Zylee decided that he wanted to take the school bus because he likes to talk with his friends on the way to school.

As we pulled up to the school my mom says, "Ok, Zolie, we are here! Now, remember what I said about being a good friend to Carmen. Let her know that we will help her family as much as we can and let her know that we will bring them all of their hygiene supplies once her mom says that it is ok."

Then I said, "Ok, mommy, I will!!" And then I grabbed Carmen's Z-Hygiene bag and jumped out of the car saying, "Thanks again, mommy, you are the best!!"

Once I got inside of the school building I went into the cafeteria and there was Carmen sitting at the table by herself drinking her milk and eating her breakfast.

I rushed right over to her saying, "Hey, Carmen!!"

And then she turned and smiled at me saying, "Hi Zolie!!" And then I said, "Carmen, I talked to my mom last night and guess what?"

Then Carmen replied, "What?" I said, "My mom got you so much stuff last night. I mean we got you a lot of stuff, but I can't bring it all to school until your mom says it's ok. But, I did bring you a smaller hygiene bag that you can use today if you want to."

And then Carmen replied with tears streaming down her face, "Thank you, Zolie. You are the best kind of friend that a girl can have. I am speechless."

And then I replied, "You're welcome Carmen, but I haven't even told you what we got for you."

And then she said, "It doesn't matter. It's just the thought, Zolie. Most people say that they will help us and don't, but you did."

Then I said, "Yeah, well, that's what friends do and besides, I just couldn't sleep at night knowing that you were living the way that you are living." I looked at the Z-Hygiene bag we got her and handed it to her saying, "This is your hygiene bag to use at school and you can leave it in your locker too.

Then she said, "It's such a pretty bag and it has my name on it. Thank you so much Zolie!!!"

And then I said, "Open it," and then she opened it and saw all of the hygiene stuff and smiled and said, "Ewww, I want to go use all of this right now."

Then I replied, "I was hoping you'd say that. Let's go to the restroom so that I can show you how to use the deodorant and you can also try on the cool headbands that we got you."

Then she said, "Ok, but first I have something to tell you." And I replied, "Ok, tell me."

And then she said, "I don't know what it is, but you must have given us good luck because yesterday my mom told me that she got a job, Zolie!! She finally got a job and now we can move into a shelter until we are able to get our own home.

And then I screamed and said, "Really?! Oh, I am so happy for you, Carmen!!!"

"We actually moved into the shelter last night," she said.

"You did!!!" I said.

Then she replied, "Yes, and as you can see, I don't smell so bad today because I was able to take a bath at the shelter last night, so I am wearing clean clothes today. They even have a place for us to wash our clothes there. I am so excited, Zolie!"

Then I said, "That is awesome news, Carmen!! I am so happy for you!!"

And then Carmen said, "I told my mom about you and I told her that you said you would help and she just told me to not get my hopes up because we have had so many people tell us that they would help us and they didn't. She did say that if you got me anything, I can keep it."

And I replied, "I am so glad that you told your mom and I am so glad that she said that I can help you."

Then Carmen said, "Well, I am very grateful, Zolie, for anything that you can do to help me. Just being a friend is the best gift that you have given me."

And then I said, "Well, I will always be your friend, Carmen, and I will help you as much as I can. I will teach you all that I am learning about hygiene too. I can make a hygiene chart for you to hang up at the shelter so that it will help you, like my hygiene chart helps me at home."

Then Carmen replied, "You would do that for me, Zolie??"

And then I said, "Of course I would. Isn't that what friends are for?!!

And she replied, "This really means a lot to me. I mean, I never thought that you would be my friend!"

Then I said, "I never thought that I would be your friend either because I never gave you a chance. I'm sorry."

Then Carmen replied, "It's ok. What matters is that we are friends now!! I feel so lucky, Zolie."

"I feel lucky too, Carmen", I replied.

And then we both smiled and she gave me a hug and said, "Thanks a lot friend. You are the best!!"

Then I said, "Anytime, friend, anytime!!"

Before we could say something else the school bell rang and we had to grab our bags and head to our separate classrooms. Before we parted, I promised Carmen that I would show her how to use her hygiene kit during our recess time and she was cool with that.

I am just so glad to know that because of my bad hygiene I was able to meet another person who had bad hygiene too, but, it was only because they couldn't help themselves like I could because they didn't have what they needed like a home or clean clothes.

Now I understand why it is so important not to be mean to people who stink because sometimes they don't know that they are stinking and sometimes they have no other choice because of their life at home.

I am so glad that my mom allowed me to help Carmen and that my mom helped me with my "bad, bad hygiene" so that I can help myself and help others. I can't wait for recess and for school to be over so that I can tell my mommy just how awesome today was.

I am so happy for Carmen and her family. They have a place to call home now. I feel really happy today and I feel grateful.

Remember to think before you judge someone because like my mommy says, you never know what a person could be going through. And be a friend because everybody needs somebody, just like my friend Carmen needed me and I need her too because my mom says good friends are hard to come by!!!

Oh, and don't forget to stay on top of your hygiene because if you can't smell yourself, then something is wrong with your nose!! ☒

Feel free to use my hygiene chart if you need a little help or just make one of your own!! Oh, and I did end up adding "deodorant" to my chart too!!

Well, I have to get to class now!!! See you in my next adventure, friends …

Love ya like sunshine!!! I'm Zolie Zi and don't you forget it!!!!!!

 Hygiene Affirmation

My Hygiene is everything. My Hygiene is me. It is up to me to keep myself clean. I am not at my best when I am not clean. So it is important to keep up with my Hygiene.

I must brush my teeth and take care of my health because no one else can do it, no, no one else. I must take baths and use soap when I do because soap makes you smell good and lotion does too.

I must also brush my hair and put on clean clothes so that I won't offend anyone at school or at home. How can I offend someone, is the question you might ask? Well, people get offended when you smell bad from not taking baths. Sometimes you can offend people when you wear dirty clothes too because the smell can be real stinky and clog up people's nose too.

I want you to pinky swear and promise with me that every day and every night you will practice having good hygiene!!! ☺

You can do it!!!

Love, Zolie Zi

A special letter from Zolie

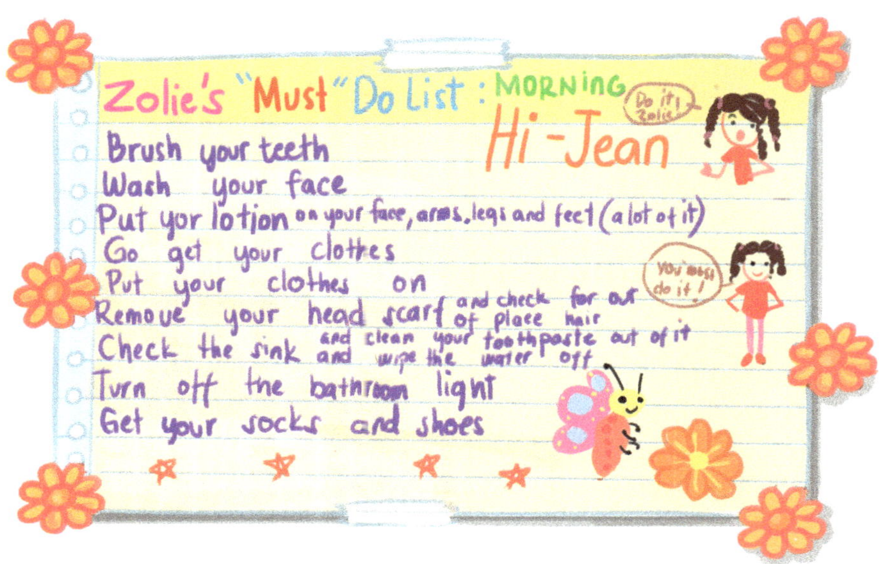

Hi Z-Friends!! Please feel free to use my morning Hygiene chart!!

You can make your own "hygiene" chart too! Make yourself a night "hygiene" chart as well, I did!

My mom said that everyone has different night hygiene routines, so you can just make one that is like your routine at home.

I hope that you are excited about your hygiene after reading my book!!

Stay Clean!!! ☺

Love,

Zolie Zi

About the Author

Sonya J. Bowser was born in Santa Fe, NM and grew up in Little Rock, AR and Austin, TX. After graduating high school, she moved to Atlanta, GA to pursue a degree in Mass Communications at Morris Brown College. Later, she took her first freelance job as a writer and editor for 12 year old Kenya James', "Blackgirl Magazine". She continued writing for several other publications and discovered a true passion for writing.

Five years later, Ms. Bowser left Atlanta to be closer to home in Dallas, Texas. She developed a passion for writing children's books and released her first book in 2006, Learning to Love Me: Self Esteem for Children. 

She has participated and spoken at Sister's Town Hall Rallies, community and recreation centers, summits, various bookstores and schools throughout America and International.

Her newest book is called "The Adventures of Zolie "Miss Chit Chat" Zi and she is excited about sharing Zolie's adventures with the children of the world.

She currently lives in Dallas, Texas.